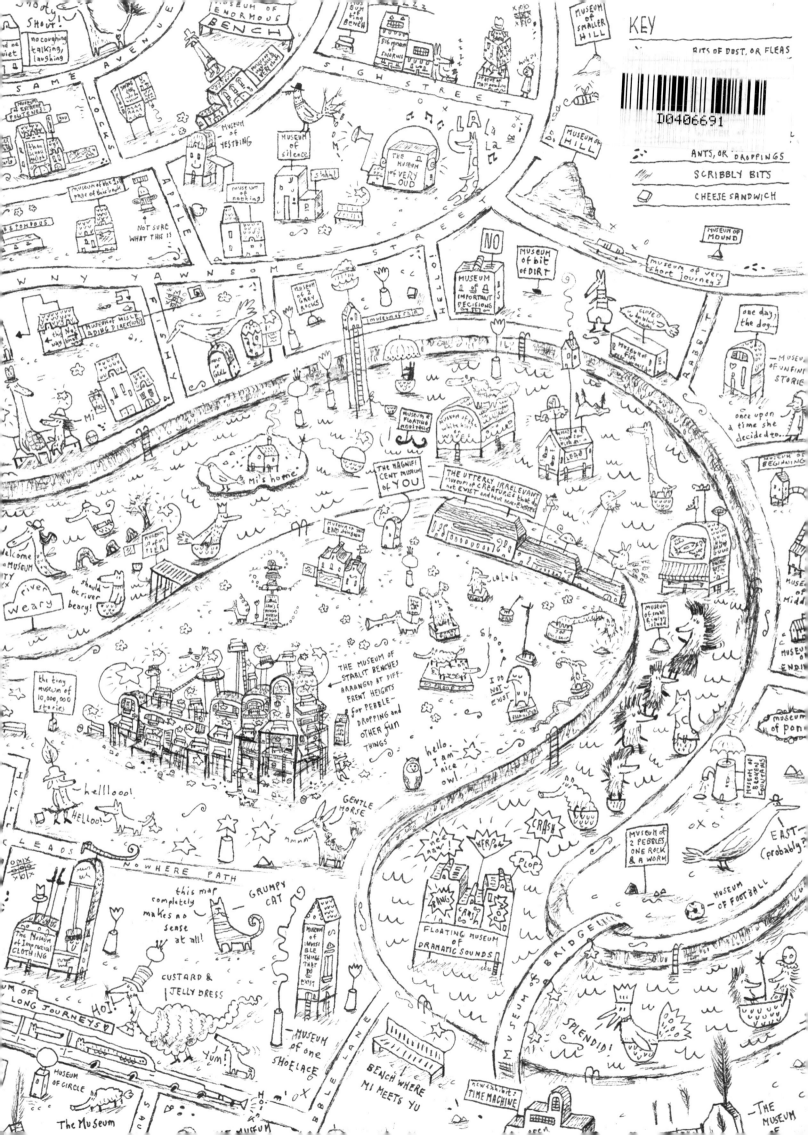

Museum City is very far north, and a little bit east.

It's been around far longer than Mi, but not much longer than Yu.

And every building in Museum City, apart from one – Mi's house – is a museum.

MUSEUM of the first Page of this book

Now showing: MIDDLES & ENDINGS

NORTH

museum of nothing

museum of uninteresting smells

PONG

YUM!

WEST (or, the previous page)

Yu

NICE-FACED LION

EXTREMELY IMPORTANT!

HELLOOO first page!

* A tiny hut in the middle of The River Weary

NOT NORTH

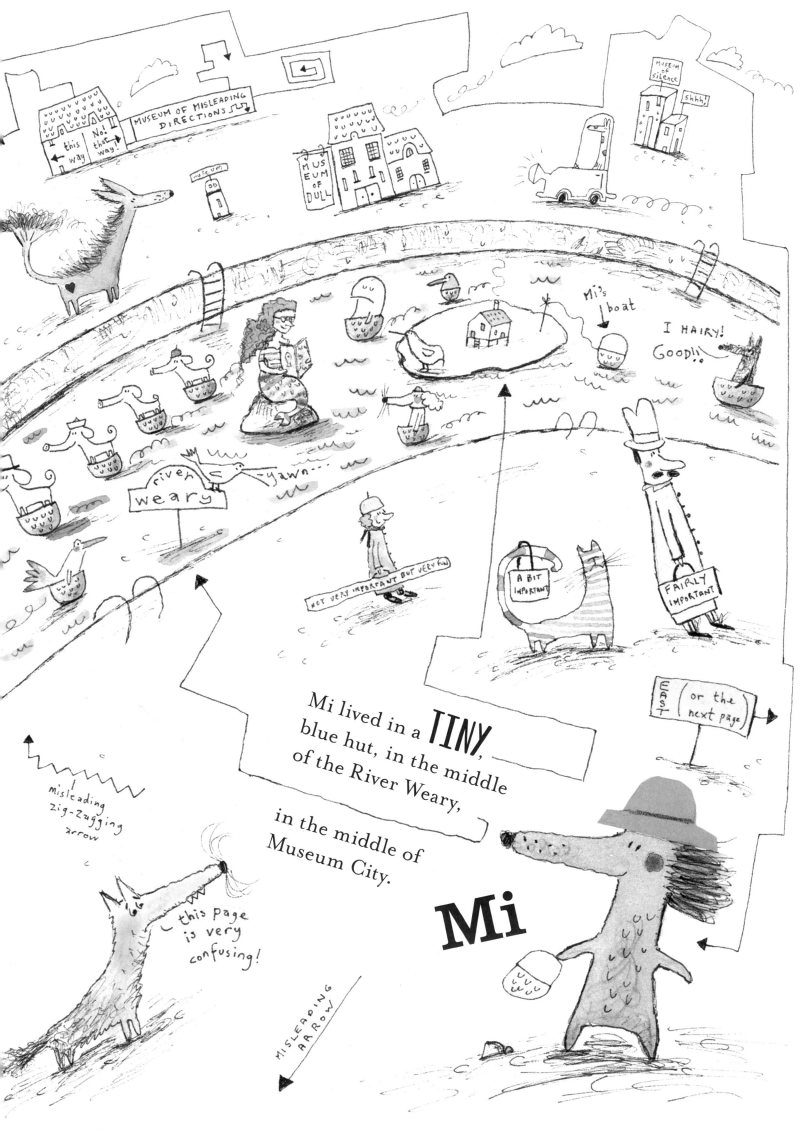

Mi lived in a **TINY**, blue hut, in the middle of the River Weary,

in the middle of Museum City.

Mi

It was a **LONELY** and **DULL** place to live, full of museums about uninteresting things and the people who owned these uninteresting things; museums about important buildings and the people who lived in these important buildings.

And although Mi quite liked a few of the museums, mostly he just felt a little bored, a little sad and a lot **LONELY**.

The two
things that *did* make
him happy were his collection
of pebbles that he loved to drop from
different heights, onto different
surfaces, to hear the sounds
they made,

and . . .

STARLIGHT!

COLLECTING pebbles, One day, while out Mi heard a new sound. Not a city sound, like fast cars and buses. No.

This was an altogether different sound. A sound like summer. A sound like happy. A sound that made Mi want to jump up and down, and run and dance, and shout,

"YES! I am Mi! Happy to be me!"

He followed **THE** sound through back streets and front streets, through up and down streets, across mountains and rivers, until he found where it was coming from.

There,
on a bench,
by the river, was a

BIG, TALL THING,
playing a huge
one-stringed instrument.
And the music it made was the
loveliest Mi had ever heard.
He sang,

"I am Mi, happy to meet you!"

And the Big Thing sang back,

"I am Yu, happy to meet Mi!"

Mi invited Yu for a picnic at his favourite place for dropping pebbles: Starlit Bench on Pebble-Drop Hill.

They ate puffy toast, drank Shlurpo, dropped pebbles and made up new songs.

That evening, Mi looked very thoughtful. He said to Yu, "You know, there should be a museum about instruments that make music like yours. And a museum about the sounds pebbles make when dropped from different heights onto different surfaces."

Yu agreed. "Let's ask the Mayor's permission to create them."

I like this **bench**! LA LA LA
it's VERY **BENCHY**! La La La
BENCHES can be **long** and STRONG,
or small **AND** also STRONG! LA LA LA
Like this SONG LA LA LA

NO

MUSEUM
of
IMPORTANT
DECISIONS

So, the next day, they
went to ask the Mayor.

But Mayor Boouf said:

"NO!

We cannot have fun things here! Museum City is a serious PLACE, for IMPORTANT and unfunny things!"

Then Mi had an idea. He climbed up Yu with his basket of pebbles and began dropping them.

Mayor Bouff looked **PUZZLED** and made a strange sound.

And Yu began playing his one-stringed instrument.

All this had a **VERY** strange
effect on the Mayor.

First, he looked confused.
Then, he started flapping his arms
and tapping his feet.

Then, he **JUMPED** up and down,
and **RAN** and **DANCED**, and **SHOUTED**,

"I am Mayor Boouf! Happy to be Me!!

And I never knew life could be SUCH FUN!

Thank you. Yes! YES!! Hmmmm. Hmmmm.

Please DO open these NEW museums!"

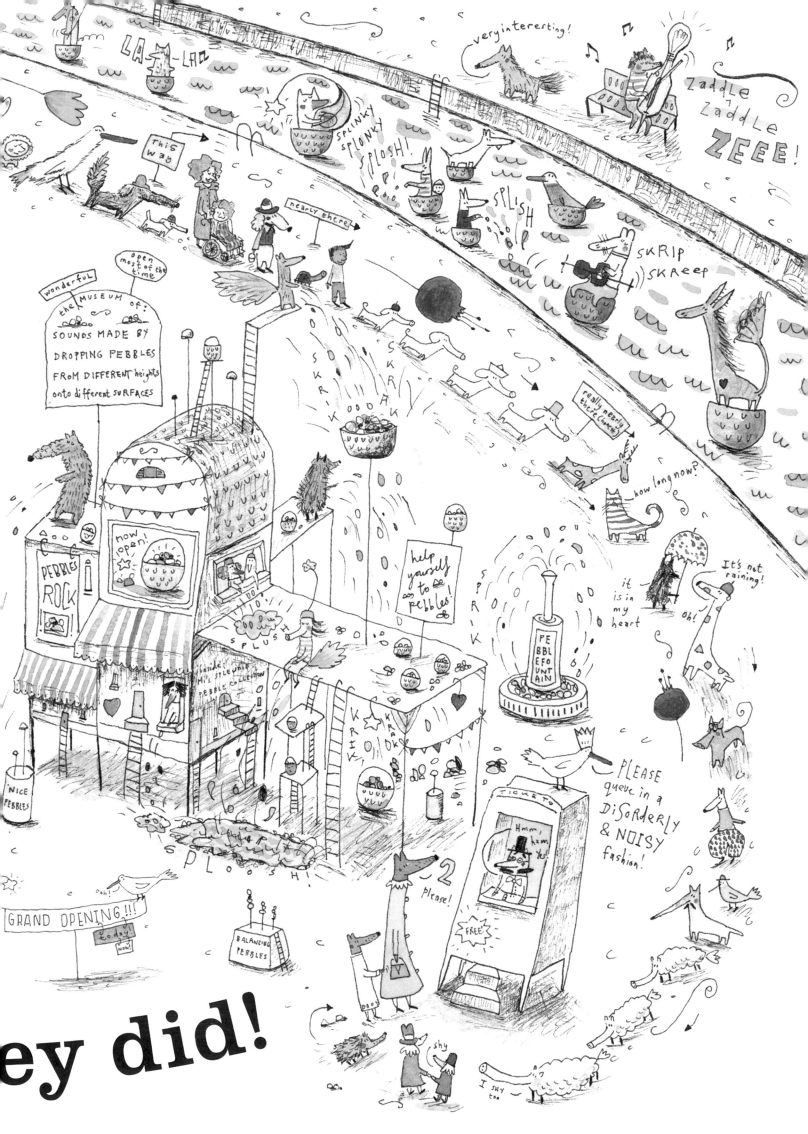

After that, with Mayor Boouf's permission, other new museums started to spring up everywhere.

The **CAT** that looked like a **DOG** opened a museum about animals like himself.

Museum of nice patch of sky

amazing!

MUSEUM OF: I'm not SURE what IT is, but it LOOKS VAGUELY INTERESTING

WEST WING

EAST WING

new exhibition: WHAT IS IT?

museum of very small journeys

A GLIMPSE inside the EAST WING

Big Hat Duck opened a museum about his collection of very interesting **(BUT VERY USELESS)** things.

LA LA LAA

Yes! it does look vaguely interesting

— floaty, fluffy, pom-pom-like thing

SPLENDID!

YES!

awesome!

— big puffy thing (or maybe hair?)

NOT SURE WHAT THIS IS ?!

DROPPED OUT OF THE SKY LAST SUMMER

SMALL, FLUFFY THING THAT HUMS

REVOLVING THING THAT LIGHTS UP IF YOU SING

BREAD -SHAPED OBJECT

SMALL DOT

YELLOW, SQUISHY THING

RANDOM OBJECTS THAT WOBBLE

BLUE THING THAT SMELLS A BIT FUNNY

STRIPEY THING

— small, lost thing

Umbrella Thing created a Museum of Rain that housed three billion

R A I n D r O p S

and one piece of lost rainbow.

And THE Bald-Headed Smoo opened a museum about creatures, like himself, that don't exist.

There were
STACKABLE museums,
and **STAIRCASEY** museums,
museums that flew, and museums that **GREW**,
and even a few about seasons.

There **WERE** museums about clothes you can wear and clothes you almost can't.

SOME SAMPLE EXHIBITS

BREAD SHOES (loafers)

CUSTARD BOOTS

JELLY AND SPONGE DRESS

WIDE-COLLAR, SMALL-WINGED COAT

— BROOM HAT (borrowed from the MUSEUM of IMPRACTICAL CLOTHING)

I still don't exist

HOINK

SOME SAMPLE EXHIBITS

SMALL BOWL OF NOTHING

ANCIENT GRAINS OF SAND

SHADOW OF KING ABSENT III

PORTRAIT OF SIR BARELY THERE (museum founder)

I'm bearly there!

— SOMETHING TOO BARELY THERE TO BE IDENTIFIED

Museums about **SMALL THINGS,** barely there things, and invisible things that do exist.

MUSEUM of invisible things **THAT DO EXIST**

NEW SHOW: wind

There!

what a silly woman! of course I exist!!

this is my invisible friend: HETTY LION

there's no such thing dear!

Helllooo!! I EXIST!!!

There were museums about everything from A to Mi.

Museum City was now a **FUN, BRIGHT,** place to live. Mi was no longer a little bored and a little sad. And he was definitely no longer lonely.

And **ALWAYS,**
before going home
at the end of every day,
he would visit his favourite place.

THE MUSEUM OF STARLIT BENCHES, ARRANGED AT DIFFERENT HEIGHTS FOR PEBBLE-DROPPING AND OTHER FUN THINGS.

THIS IS A COPY OF
THE MAP of MUSEUM CITY
THAT CAN BE BOUGHT from
the MUSEUM of UPSIDE
DOWN and BACK to FRONT